The Christopher Robin
Story Book

The Christopher Robin Story Book

from

WHEN WE WERE VERY YOUNG, NOW WE
ARE SIX, WINNIE-THE-POOH AND
THE HOUSE AT POOH CORNER

by

A. A. MILNE

illustrated by

E. H. SHEPARD

METHUEN CHILDREN'S BOOKS
LONDON

First published October 31, 1929
by Methuen & Co Ltd
Reprinted twenty-seven times
Reprinted 1975 by Methuen Children's Books Ltd,
11 New Fetter Lane, London EC4P 4EE
Reprinted 1977
Printed in Great Britain by
Whitstable Litho Ltd, Whitstable, Kent

ISBN 0 416 31170 9

THE AUTHOR TO HIS READERS

YOU will find here a collection of verses and stories, mostly about a little boy called Christopher Robin. The verses are taken from two books of mine called *When We Were Very Young* and *Now We Are Six* ; and the stories are taken from two other books called *Winnie-the-Pooh* and *The House at Pooh Corner*. I began to write the first book when Christopher Robin was three years old, and I finished writing the last one when he was just eight, so you mustn't expect him always to seem the same age to you as you read. Like most little boys, he has had toy animals to play with, but though he loves them all, his best friend has been his Teddy Bear, called Winnie-the-Pooh, or Pooh, for short. The funny thing is that Pooh doesn't like being called a Teddy Bear now, and if anybody says to Christopher Robin, ' Is that your T——y B——? ' Christopher Robin says very coldly, ' No, it's Pooh,' and then Pooh and he go off whispering together. You see, what they both feel and what I feel too, is that Pooh is really alive and does things, but a Teddy Bear is just a toy which sits about and does nothing ; and we feel that anybody who could see Pooh, if only for a moment, and not know at once that he was alive, must be a very silly person.

Well, the stories in this book are about the adventures which Pooh and his friends have in the Forest with Christopher Robin. And though some of the verses seem to be about some other little boy or girl, yet this one little boy was always in my mind when I wrote them. Even when I wrote about Kings and Queens (as you will see that I have) I tried to write about them as Christopher Robin would think about them. So it is really as if all the time he had been telling me what to say, and I had been writing it down in verse for him.

Now I must just say something about verses and poetry, and then you can get on with the book. I expect you have danced sometimes, or seen other people dancing, and you know that when you dance you have to ' keep time ' to the music. Even if there is no music playing, you can hum a tune to yourself as you dance (without anybody hearing) and keep time to that. Now you know, of course, that verses have rhymes in them ; but even more important than the rhymes is what is called the ' rhythm '. It is a difficult-looking word, but what it means is just ' the time that the verse keeps '. Every piece of poetry has a music of its own which it is humming to itself as it goes along, and every line, every word, in it has to keep time to this music. That is what makes it difficult to write poetry : because you can't use just any words in any order, as long as it's sense and grammar, but you have to use particular words in a particular order, so that they keep time to the music and rhyme when you want them to. If you can find words which keep time to the music, and which are just the words for what you want to say, then the verses which you write are verses which sing themselves into people's heads and stay there for ever, so that even when they are alone and unhappy they have this music with them for company.

So if you like learning these verses and find them easy to remember, I shall be very glad, because it will mean that I wrote them the right way. But if you don't, I shall be very sorry.

A. A. MILNE

CONTENTS

* This poem, being in the Library of the Queen's Dolls' House, is printed here by special permission.

The Christopher Robin
Story Book

HOPPITY

CHRISTOPHER ROBIN goes
Hoppity, hoppity,

Hoppity, hoppity, hop.
Whenever I tell him
Politely to stop it, he
Says he can't possibly stop.

If he stopped hopping, he couldn't go anywhere,
Poor little Christopher
Couldn't go anywhere . . .
That's why he *always* goes
Hoppity, hoppity,
Hoppity,
Hoppity,
Hop.

TEDDY BEAR

A BEAR, however hard he tries,
Grows tubby without exercise.
Our Teddy Bear is short and fat
Which is not to be wondered at ;
He gets what exercise he can
By falling off the ottoman,
But generally seems to lack
The energy to clamber back.

Now tubbiness is just the thing
Which gets a fellow wondering ;
And Teddy worried lots about
The fact that he was rather stout.

He thought : ' If only I were thin !
But how does anyone begin ? '
He thought : ' It really isn't fair
To grudge me exercise and air.'

For many weeks he pressed in vain
His nose against the window-pane,
And envied those who walked about
Reducing their unwanted stout.
None of the people he could see
' Is quite ' (he said) ' as fat as me ! '
Then, with a still more moving sigh,
' I mean ' (he said) ' as fat as I ! '

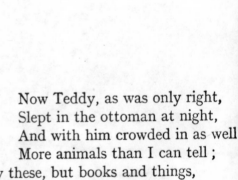

Now Teddy, as was only right,
Slept in the ottoman at night,
And with him crowded in as well
More animals than I can tell ;
Not only these, but books and things,
Such as a kind relation brings—
Old tales of ' Once upon a time ',
And history retold in rhyme.

One night it happened that he took
A peep at an old picture-book,
Wherein he came across by chance
The picture of a King of France
(A stoutish man) and, down below,
These words : ' King Louis So and So,
Nicknamed " The Handsome ! " ' There he sat,
And (think of it !) the man was fat !

Our bear rejoiced like anything
To read about this famous King,
Nicknamed ' The Handsome.' There he sat,
And certainly the man was fat.
Nicknamed ' The Handsome.' Not a doubt
The man was definitely stout.
Why then, a bear (for all his tub)
Might yet be named ' The Handsome Cub !

' Might yet be named.'   Or did he mean
That years ago he ' might have been ? '
For now he felt a slight misgiving :
' Is Louis So and So still living ?
Fashions in beauty have a way
Of altering from day to day.
Is " Handsome Louis " with us yet ?
Unfortunately I forget.'

Next morning (nose to window-pane)
The doubt occurred to him again.
One question hammered in his head :
' Is he alive or is he dead ? '
Thus, nose to pane, he pondered ; but
The lattice window, loosely shut,
Swung open.   With one startled ' Oh ! '
Our Teddy disappeared below.

There happened to be passing by
A plump man with a twinkling eye,
Who, seeing Teddy in the street,
Raised him politely to his feet,
And murmured kindly in his ear
Soft words of comfort and of cheer :
' Well, well ! '   ' Allow me ! '   ' Not at all.'
' Tut-tut !   A very nasty fall.'

Our Teddy answered not a word ;
It's doubtful if he even heard.
Our bear could only look and look :
The stout man in the picture-book !
That ' handsome ' King—could this be he,
This man of adiposity ?
' Impossible,' he thought.   ' But still,
No harm in asking.   Yes, I will ! '

' Are you,' he said, ' by any chance
His Majesty the King of France ? '
The other answered, ' I am that,'
Bowed stiffly, and removed his hat ;
Then said, ' Excuse me,' with an air,
' But is it Mr. Edward Bear ? '
And Teddy, bending very low,
Replied politely, ' Even so ! '

They stood beneath the window there,
The King and Mr. Edward Bear,
And, handsome, if a trifle fat,
Talked carelessly of this and that. . . .
Then said His Majesty, ' Well, well,
I must get on,' and rang the bell.
' Your bear, I think,' he smiled. ' Good-day!'
And turned and went upon his way.

A bear, however hard he tries,
Grows tubby without exercise.
Our Teddy Bear is short and fat,
Which is not to be wondered at.
But do you think it worries him
To know that he is far from slim ?
No, just the other way about—
He's *proud* of being short and stout.

IN WHICH WE ARE INTRODUCED TO WINNIE-THE-POOH AND SOME BEES, AND THE STORIES BEGIN

HERE is Edward Bear, coming downstairs now, bump, bump, bump, on the back of his head, behind Christopher Robin. It is, as far as he knows, the only way of coming downstairs, but sometimes he feels that there really is another way, if only he could stop bumping for a moment and think of it. And then he feels that perhaps there isn't. Anyhow, here he is at the bottom, and ready to be introduced to you. Winnie-the-Pooh.

When I first heard his name, I said, just as you are going to say, ' But I thought he was a boy ? '

' So did I,' said Christopher Robin.

' Then you can't call him Winnie ? '

' I don't.'

' But you said——'

' He's Winnie-ther-Pooh. Don't you know what " *ther* " means ? '

'Ah, yes, now I do,' I said quickly ; and I hope you do too, because it is all the explanation you are going to get.

Sometimes Winnie-the-Pooh likes a game of some sort when he comes downstairs, and sometimes he likes to sit quietly in front of the fire and listen to a story.   This evening——

'What about a story ? ' said Christopher Robin.

'*What* about a story ? ' I said.

'Could you very sweetly tell Winnie-the-Pooh one ? '

'I suppose I could,' I said.   'What sort of stories does he like ? '

'About himself.   Because he's *that* sort of Bear.'

'Oh, I see.'

'So could you very sweetly ? '

'I'll try,' I said.

So I tried.

.   •   ⸳   -   •

Once upon a time, a very long time ago now, about last Friday, Winnie-the-Pooh lived in a forest all by himself under the name of Sanders.

('*What does " under the name " mean ?*' asked
Christopher Robin.

'*It means he had the name over the door in gold
letters, and lived under it.*'

'*Winnie-the-Pooh wasn't quite sure,*' said
Christopher Robin.

'*Now I am,*' said a growly voice.

'*Then I will go on,*' said I.)

One day when he was out walking, he came to an open place in the middle of the forest, and in the middle of this place was a large oak-tree, and, from the top of the tree, there came a loud buzzing-noise.

Winnie-the-Pooh sat down at the foot of the tree, put his head between his paws and began to think.

First of all he said to himself: 'That noise means something. You don't get a buzzing-noise like that, just buzzing and buzzing, without its meaning something. If there's a buzzing-noise, somebody's making a buzzing-noise, and the only reason for making a buzzing-noise that *I* know of is because you're a bee.'

Then he thought another long time, and said : 'And the only reason for being a bee that I know of is making honey.'

And then he got up, and said : 'And the only reason for making honey is so as *I* can eat it.' So he began to climb the tree.

He
climbed
and
he
climbed
and
he
climbed,
and
as
he
climbed
he
sang
a
little
song
to
himself.
It
went
like
this :

Isn't it funny
How a bear likes honey ?
Buzz ! Buzz ! Buzz !
I wonder why he does ?

Then he climbed a little farther . . . and a

little farther . . . and then just a little farther.
By that time he had thought of another song.

> It's a very funny thought that, if Bears were Bees,
> They'd build their nests at the *bottom* of trees.
> And that being so (if the Bees were Bears),
> We shouldn't have to climb up all these stairs.

He was getting rather
tired by this time, so that
is why he sang a Com-
plaining Song.   He was
nearly there now, and if
he just stood on that
branch. . . .
   Crack !
' Oh, help ! ' said Pooh, as he dropped ten feet
on to the branch below him.

' If only I hadn't——' he said, as he bounced twenty feet on to the next branch.

' You see, what I *meant* to do,' he explained, as he turned head-over-heels, and crashed on to another branch thirty feet below, ' what I *meant* to do——'

' Of course, it *was* rather——' he admitted, as he slithered very quickly through the next six branches.

' It all comes, I suppose,' he decided, as he said good-bye to the last branch, spun round three times, and flew gracefully into a gorse-bush, ' it all comes of *liking* honey so much. Oh, help ! '

He crawled out of the gorse-bush, brushed the prickles from his nose, and began to think again. And the first person he thought of was Christopher Robin.

(' *Was that me ? ' said Christopher Robin in an awed voice, hardly daring to believe it.*

' *That was you.*'

Christopher Robin said nothing, but his eyes got larger and larger, and his face got pinker and pinker.)

So Winnie-the-Pooh went round to his friend Christopher Robin, who lived behind a green door in another part of the forest.

' Good morning, Christopher Robin,' he said.

' Good morning, Winnie-*ther*-Pooh,' said you.

' I wonder if you've got such a thing as a balloon about you ? '

' A balloon ? '

' Yes, I just said to myself coming along : " I wonder if Christopher Robin has such a thing as a balloon about him ? " I just said it to my-self, thinking of balloons, and wondering.'

' What do you want a balloon for ? ' you said.

Winnie-the-Pooh looked round to see that nobody was listening, put his paw to his mouth, and said in a deep whisper : ' *Honey !* '

' But you don't get honey with balloons ! '

' *I* do,' said Pooh.

Well, it just happened that you had been to a party the day before at the house of your friend Piglet, and you had balloons at the party. You had had a big green balloon ; and one of Rabbit's relations had had a big blue one, and had left it behind, being really too young to go to a party at all ; and so you had brought the green one *and* the blue one home with you.

' Which one would you like? ' you asked Pooh.

He put his head between his paws and thought very carefully.

' It's like this,' he said. ' When you go after honey with a balloon, the great thing is not to let the bees know you're coming. Now, if you have a green balloon, they might think you were only part of the tree, and not notice you, and if you have a blue balloon, they might think you were only part of the sky, and not notice you, and the question is : Which is most likely ? '

' Wouldn't they notice *you* underneath the balloon ? ' you asked.

' They might or they might not,' said Winnie-the-Pooh. ' You never can tell with bees.' He thought for a moment and said : ' I shall try to look like a small black cloud. That will deceive them.'

' Then you had better have the blue balloon,' you said ; and so it was decided.

Well, you both went out with the blue balloon, and you took your gun with you, just in case, as you always did, and Winnie-the-Pooh went to a

very muddy place that he knew of, and rolled
and rolled until he was black all over ; and then,
when the balloon was blown up as big as big,
and you and Pooh were both holding on to the
string, you let go suddenly, and Pooh Bear
floated gracefully up into the sky, and stayed
there—level with the top of the tree and about
twenty feet away from it.

' Hooray ! ' you shouted.

' Isn't that fine ? ' shouted Winnie-the-Pooh
down to you.   ' What do I look like ? '

' You look like a Bear holding on to a balloon,' you said.

' Not,' said Pooh anxiously, '—not like a small
black cloud in a blue sky ? '

' Not very much.'

' Ah, well, perhaps from up here it looks
different.   And as I say, you never can tell with
bees.'

There was no wind to blow him nearer to the
tree, so there he stayed.   He could see the
honey, he could smell the honey, but he couldn't
quite reach the honey.

After a little while he called down to you.

'Christopher Robin!' he said in a loud whisper.

'Hallo!'

'I think the bees *suspect* something!'

'What sort of thing?'

'I don't know. But something tells me that

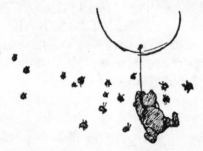

they're *suspicious*!'

'Perhaps they think that you're after their honey.'

'It may be that. You never can tell with bees.'

There was another little silence, and then he called down to you again.

'Christopher Robin!'

'Yes?'

'Have you an umbrella in your house?'

'I think so.'

'I wish you would bring it out here, and walk up and down with it, and look up at me every now and then, and say ' Tut-tut, it looks like rain.' I think, if you did that, it would help the deception which we are practising on these bees.'

Well, you laughed to yourself, ' Silly old Bear ! ' but you didn't say it aloud because you were so fond of him, and you went home for your umbrella.

' Oh, there you are ! ' called down Winnie-the-Pooh, as soon as you got back to the tree. ' I was beginning to get anxious. I have discovered that the bees are now definitely Suspicious.'

' Shall I put my umbrella up ? ' you said.

' Yes, but wait a moment. We must be practical. The important bee to deceive is the Queen Bee. Can you see which is the Queen Bee from down there ? '

' No.

' A pity. Well, now, if you walk up and down with your umbrella, saying, " Tut-tut, it looks like rain," I shall do what I can by singing a little cloud Song, such as a cloud might sing. . . . Go ! '

So, while you walked up and down and wondered if it would rain, Winnie-the-Pooh sang this song :

> How sweet to be a Cloud
>   Floating in the Blue !
> Every little cloud
> *Always* sings aloud,

> ' How sweet to be a Cloud
>   Floating in the Blue ! '
> It makes him very proud
> To be a little cloud.

The bees were still buzzing as suspiciously as ever. Some of them, indeed, left their nests and flew all round the cloud as it began the

second verse of this song, and one bee sat down
on the nose of the cloud for a moment, and then
got up again.

'Christopher—*ow !*—Robin,' called out the
cloud.

'Yes ? '

'I have just been thinking, and I have come
to a very important decision. *These are the
wrong sort of bees.*'

'Are they ? '

'Quite the wrong sort. So I should think
they would make the wrong sort of honey,
shouldn't you ? '

'Would they ? '

'Yes. So I think I shall come down.'

'How ? ' asked you.

Winnie-the-Pooh hadn't thought about this.
If he let go the string, he would fall—*bump*—
and he didn't like the idea of that. So he
thought for a long time, and then he said :

'Christopher Robin, you must shoot the
balloon with your gun. Have you got your gun ? '

'Of course I have,' you said. 'But if I do
that, it will spoil the balloon,' you said.

' But if you *don't*,' said Pooh, ' I shall have to let go, and that would spoil *me*.'

When he put it like this, you saw how it was, and you aimed very carefully at the balloon, and fired.

' *Ow !* ' said Pooh.

' Did I miss ? ' you asked.

' You didn't exactly *miss*,' said Pooh, ' but you missed the *balloon*.'

' I'm so sorry,' you said, and you fired again

and this time you hit the balloon, and the air came slowly out, and Winnie-the-Pooh floated down to the ground.

But his arms were so stiff from holding on to the string of the balloon all that time that they stayed up straight in the air for more than a week, and whenever a fly came and settled on his nose he had to blow it off. And I think— but I am not sure—that *that* is why he was always called Pooh.

. . . . .

' Is that the end of the story ? ' asked Christopher Robin.

' That's the end of that one. There are others.'

' About Pooh and Me ? '

' And Piglet and Rabbit and all of you. Don't you remember ? '

' I do remember, and then when I try to remember, I forget.'

' That day when Pooh and Piglet tried to catch the Heffalump——'

' They didn't catch it, did they ? '

' No.'

' Pooh couldn't, because he hasn't any brain. Did *I* catch it ? '

' Well, that comes into the story.'

Christopher Robin nodded.

' I do remember,' he said, ' only Pooh doesn't very well so that's why he likes having it told to him again. Because then it's a real story and not just a remembering.'

' That's just how *I* feel,' I said.

Christopher Robin gave a deep sigh, picked his Bear up by the leg, and walked off to the door, trailing Pooh behind him. At the door

he turned and said, ' Coming to see me have my bath ? '

' I might,' I said.

' I didn't hurt him when I shot him, did I ? '

' Not a bit.'

He nodded and went out, and in a moment I heard Winnie-the-Pooh—*bump, bump, bump*—going up the stairs behind him.

HALFWAY DOWN

HALFWAY DOWN

HALFWAY down the stairs
Is a stair
Where I sit.
There isn't any
Other stair
Quite like
It.
I'm not at the bottom,
I'm not at the top ;
So this is the stair
Where
I always
Stop.

Halfway up the stairs
Isn't up,
And isn't down.
It isn't in the nursery,
It isn't in the town.
And all sorts of funny thoughts
Run round my head :
' It isn't really
Anywhere !
It's somewhere else
Instead ! '

LINES AND SQUARES

WHENEVER I walk in a London street,
I'm ever so careful to watch my feet;
    And I keep in the squares,
    And the masses of bears,

Who wait at the corners all ready to eat
The sillies who tread on the lines of the street,
   Go back to their lairs,
   And I say to them, ' Bears,
   Just look how I'm walking in all of the
                     squares ! '

And the little bears growl to each other, ' He's mine,
As soon as he's silly and steps on a line.'
And some of the bigger bears try to pretend
That they came round the corner to look for a friend ;
And they try to pretend that nobody cares
Whether you walk on the lines or squares.
But only the sillies believe their talk ;
It's ever so portant how you walk.
And it's ever so jolly to call out, ' Bears,
Just watch me walking in all the squares ! '

DISOBEDIENCE

JAMES James
Morrison Morrison
Weatherby George Dupree
Took great
Care of his Mother,
Though he was only three.

James James
Said to his Mother,
'Mother,' he said, said he;
'You must never go down to the end of the
town, if you don't go down with me.'

James James
Morrison's Mother
Put on a golden gown.
James James
Morrison's Mother
Drove to the end of the town.

James James
Morrison's Mother
Said to herself, said she :
' I can get right down to the end of the town
and be back in time for tea.'

King John
Put up a notice,
' LOST or STOLEN or STRAYED !
JAMES JAMES
MORRISON'S MOTHER
SEEMS TO HAVE BEEN MISLAID.
LAST SEEN
WANDERING VAGUELY :
QUITE OF HER OWN ACCORD,
SHE TRIED TO GET DOWN TO THE END
OF THE TOWN—FORTY SHILLINGS
REWARD !'

James James
Morrison Morrison
(Commonly known as Jim)
Told his
Other relations
Not to go blaming *him*.

James James
Said to his Mother,
' Mother,' he said, said he ;
' You must *never* go down to the end of the
town without consulting me.'

James James
Morrison's Mother
Hasn't been heard of since.
King John
Said he was sorry,
So did the Queen and Prince.
King John
(Somebody told me)
Said to a man he knew :
' If people go down to the end of the town, well,
    what can *anyone* do ? '

(*Now then, very softly*)

    J. J.
    M. M.
    W. G. Du P.
    Took great
    C/o his M*****
    Though he was only 3.
    J. J.
    Said to his M*****
    ' M*****,' he said, said he :
' You-must-never-go-down-to-the-end-of-the-
    town-if-you-don't-go-down-with ME ! '

IN WHICH POOH AND PIGLET GO HUNT-
ING AND NEARLY CATCH A WOOZLE

THE Piglet lived in a very grand house in the middle of a beech-tree, and the beech-tree was in the middle of the forest, and the Piglet lived in the middle of the house. Next to his house was a piece of broken board which had : ' TRESPASSERS W ' on it. When Christopher Robin asked the Piglet what it meant, he said it was his grandfather's name, and had been in the family for a long time. Christopher Robin said you *couldn't* be called Trespassers W, and Piglet said yes, you could, because his grandfather was, and it was short for Trespassers Will, which was short for Trespassers William. And his grandfather had had two names in case he lost one—Trespassers after an uncle, and William after Trespassers.

' I've got two names,' said Christopher Robin carelessly.

' Well, there you are, that proves it,' said Piglet.

One fine winter's day when Piglet was brushing away the snow in front of his house, he

happened to look up, and there was Winnie-the-Pooh. Pooh was walking round and round in a circle, thinking of something else, and when Piglet called to him, he just went on walking.

'Hallo!' said Piglet, 'what are *you* doing?'

'Hunting,' said Pooh.

'Hunting what?'

'Tracking something,' said Winnie-the-Pooh very mysteriously.

'Tracking what?' said Piglet, coming closer.

'That's just what I ask myself. I ask myself, What?'

'What do you think you'll answer?'

'I shall have to wait until I catch up with it,' said Winnie-the-Pooh. 'Now, look there.'

He pointed to the ground in front of him. 'What do you see there?'

'Tracks,' said Piglet. 'Paw-marks.' He gave a little squeak of excitement. 'Oh, Pooh! Do you think it's a—a—a Woozle?'

'It may be,' said Pooh. 'Sometimes it is, and sometimes it isn't. You never can tell with paw-marks.'

With these few words he went on tracking, and Piglet, after watching him for a minute or two, ran after him. Winnie-the-Pooh had come

to a sudden stop, and was bending over the tracks in a puzzled sort of way.

' What's the matter ? ' asked Piglet.

' It's a very funny thing,' said Bear, ' but there

seem to be *two* animals now. This—whatever-
it-was—has been joined by another—whatever-
it-is—and the two of them are now proceeding
in company. Would you mind coming with
me, Piglet, in case they turn out to be Hostile
Animals ? '

Piglet scratched his ear in a nice sort of way,
and said that he had nothing to do until Friday,
and would be delighted to come, in case it really
was a Woozle.

' You mean, in case it really is two Woozles,'
said Winnie-the-Pooh, and Piglet said that anyhow he had nothing to do until Friday. So off
they went together.

There was a small spinney of larch trees just
here, and it seemed as if the two Woozles, if
that is what they were, had been going round
this spinney ; so round this spinney went Pooh
and Piglet after them ; Piglet passing the time
by telling Pooh what his Grandfather Trespassers W had done to Remove Stiffness after
Tracking, and how his Grandfather Trespassers
W had suffered in his later years from Shortness
of Breath, and other matters of interest, and
Pooh wondering what a Grandfather was like,
and if perhaps this was Two Grandfathers they
were after now, and, if so, whether he would be
allowed to take one home and keep it, and what

Christopher Robin would say. And still the tracks went on in front of them. . . .

Suddenly Winnie-the-Pooh stopped, and pointed excitedly in front of him. '*Look!*'

'*What?*' said Piglet, with a jump. And then, to show that he hadn't been frightened, he jumped up and down once or twice more in an exercising sort of way.

'The tracks!' said Pooh. '*A third animal has joined the other two!*'

'Pooh!' cried Piglet. 'Do you think it is another Woozle?'

'No,' said Pooh, 'because it makes different marks. It is either Two Woozles and one, as it might be, Wizzle, or Two, as it might be, Wizzles and one, if so it is, Woozle. Let us continue to follow them.'

So they went on, feeling just a little anxious now, in case the three animals in front of them were of Hostile Intent.   And Piglet wished very much that his Grandfather T. W. were there, instead of elsewhere, and Pooh thought how nice it would be if they met Christopher Robin suddenly but quite accidentally, and only because he liked Christopher Robin so much. And then, all of a sudden, Winnie-the-Pooh stopped again, and licked the tip of his nose in

a cooling manner, for he was feeling more hot and anxious than ever in his life before. *There were four animals in front of them !*

' Do you see, Piglet ?   Look at their tracks ! Three, as it were, Woozles, and one, as it was, Wizzle. *Another Woozle has joined them !* '

And so it seemed to be. There were the tracks ; crossing over each other here, getting muddled up with each other there ; but, quite plainly every now and then, the tracks of four sets of paws.

' I *think*,' said Piglet, when he had licked the tip of his nose too, and found that it brought very little comfort, ' I *think* that I have just remembered something. I have just remembered something that I forgot to do yesterday and shan't be able to do to-morrow. So I suppose I really ought to go back and do it now.

' We'll do it this afternoon, and I'll come with you,' said Pooh.

' It isn't the sort of thing you can do in the afternoon,' said Piglet quickly. ' It's a very particular morning thing, that has to be done in the morning, and, if possible, between the hours of—— What would you say the time was ? '

' About twelve,' said Winnie-the-Pooh, looking at the sun.

' Between, as I was saying, the hours of twelve and twelve five. So, really, dear old Pooh, if you'll excuse me—— *What's that ?* '

Pooh looked up at the sky, and then, as he heard the whistle again, he looked up into the branches of a big oak-tree and then he saw a friend of his.

' It's Christopher Robin,' he said.

' Ah, then you'll be all right,' said Piglet. ' You'll be quite safe with *him*. Good-bye,' and he trotted off home as quickly as he could, very glad to be Out of All Danger again.

Christopher Robin came slowly down his tree.

' Silly old Bear,' he said, ' what *were* you doing ? First you went round the spinney twice by yourself, and then Piglet ran after you and you went round again together, and then you were just going round a fourth time——'

' Wait a moment,' said Winnie-the-Pooh, holding up his paw.

He sat down and thought, in the most

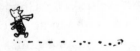

thoughtful way he could think. Then he fitted his paw into one of the Tracks . . . and then he scratched his nose twice, and stood up.

' Yes,' said Winnie-the-Pooh.

' I see now,' said Winnie-the-Pooh.

' I have been Foolish and Deluded,' said he, ' and I am a Bear of No Brain at All.'

' You're the Best Bear in All the World,' said Christopher Robin soothingly.

' Am I ? ' said Pooh hopefully. And then he brightened up suddenly.

' Anyhow,' he said, ' it is nearly Luncheon Time.'

So he went home for it.

HAPPINESS

John had
Great Big
Waterproof
Boots on ;
John had a
Great Big
Waterproof
Hat ;

John had a
Great Big
Waterproof
Mackintosh—
And that
(Said John)
Is
That.

BUCKINGHAM PALACE

THEY'RE changing guard at Buckingham Palace—
Christopher Robin went down with Alice.
Alice is marrying one of the guard.
' A soldier's life is terrible hard,'

Says Alice.

They're changing guard at Buckingham Palace—
Christopher Robin went down with Alice.
We saw a guard in a sentry-box.
' One of the sergeants looks after their socks,'

Says Alice.

They're changing guard at Buckingham Palace—
Christopher Robin went down with Alice.
We looked for the King, but he never came.
' Well, God take care of him, all the same,'

Says Alice.

They're changing guard at Buckingham Palace—
Christopher Robin went down with Alice.
They've great big parties inside the grounds.
' I wouldn't be King for a hundred pounds,'
Says Alice.

They're changing guard at Buckingham Palace—
Christopher Robin went down with Alice.
A face looked out, but it wasn't the King's.
' He's much too busy a-signing things,'
Says Alice.

They're changing guard at Buckingham Palace—
Christopher Robin went down with Alice.
' Do you think the King knows all about *me* ? '
' Sure to, dear, but it's time for tea,'
Says Alice.

THE KING'S BREAKFAST

THE King asked
The Queen, and
The Queen asked
The Dairymaid :
' Could we have some butter for
The Royal slice of bread ? '
The Queen asked
The Dairymaid,
The Dairymaid
Said, ' Certainly,
I'll go and tell
The cow
Now
Before she goes to bed.'

The Dairymaid
She curtsied,

And went and told
The Alderney :
' Don't forget the butter for
The Royal slice of bread.'

The Alderney
Said sleepily :
' You'd better tell
His Majesty

That many people nowadays
Like marmalade
Instead.'

The Dairymaid
Said, ' Fancy ! '

And went to
Her Majesty.
She curtsied to the Queen, and
She turned a little red :
' Excuse me,
Your Majesty,
For taking of
The liberty,
But marmalade is tasty, if
It's very
Thickly
Spread.'

The Queen said,
' Oh ! '
And went to
His Majesty :
' Talking of the butter for
The Royal slice of bread,
Many people
Think that

Marmalade
Is nicer.
Would you like to try a little
Marmalade
Instead ? '

The King said,
' Bother ! '
And then he said,
' Oh, deary me ! '
The King sobbed, ' Oh, deary me ! '
And went back to bed.
' Nobody,'
He whimpered,
' Could call me
A fussy man ;
I *only* want
A little bit
Of butter for
My bread ! '

The Queen said,
' There, there ! '
And went to
The Dairymaid.
The Dairymaid
Said, ' There, there ! '
And went to the shed.

The cow said,
' There, there !
I didn't really
Mean it ;
Here's milk for his porringer
And butter for his bread.'

The Queen took
The butter
And brought it to
His Majesty ;
The King said,
' Butter, eh ? '
And bounced out of bed.
' Nobody,' he said,
As he kissed her
Tenderly,
' Nobody,' he said,

As he slid down
The banisters,
' Nobody,
My darling,
Could call me
A fussy man—

BUT

' I do like a little bit of butter to my bread !'

IN WHICH EEYORE LOSES A TAIL
AND POOH FINDS ONE

THE Old Grey Donkey, Eeyore, stood by
himself in a thistly corner of the forest,
his front feet well apart, his head on one
side, and thought about things. Sometimes, he

thought sadly to himself, ' Why ? ' and sometimes he thought, ' Wherefore ? ' and sometimes
he thought, ' Inasmuch as which ? '—and sometimes he didn't quite know what he *was* thinking

about. So when Winnie-the-Pooh came stumping along, Eeyore was very glad to be able to stop thinking for a little, in order to say ' How do you do ? ' in a gloomy manner to him.

' And how are you ? ' said Winnie-the-Pooh. Eeyore shook his head from side to side.

' Not very how,' he said. ' I don't seem to have felt at all how for a long time.'

' Dear, dear,' said Pooh, ' I'm sorry about that. Let's have a look at you.'

So Eeyore stood there, gazing sadly at the ground, and Winnie-the-Pooh walked all round him once.

' Why, what's happened to your tail ? ' he said in surprise.

' What *has* happened to it ? ' said Eeyore.

' It isn't there ! '

'Are you sure?'

'Well, either a tail *is* there or it isn't there. You can't make a mistake about it. And yours *isn't* there!'

'Then what is?'

'Nothing.'

'Let's have a look,' said Eeyore, and he turned slowly round to the place where his tail had been a little while ago, and then, finding that he couldn't catch it up, he turned round the other way, until he came back to where he was at first, and then he put his head down and looked between his front legs, and at last he said, with a long, sad sigh, ' I believe you're right.'

'Of course I'm right,' said Pooh.

'That Accounts for a Good Deal,' said Eeyore gloomily. 'It Explains Everything. No Wonder.'

'You must have left it somewhere,' said Winnie-the-Pooh.

'Somebody must have taken it,' said Eeyore. 'How Like Them,' he added, after a long silence.

Pooh felt that he ought to say something helpful about it, but didn't quite know what. So he decided to do something helpful instead.

'Eeyore,' he said solemnly, 'I, Winnie-the-Pooh, will find your tail for you.'

'Thank you, Pooh,' answered Eeyore. 'You're a real friend,' said he. 'Not like Some,' he said.

So Winnie-the-Pooh went off to find Eeyore's tail.

It was a fine spring morning in the forest as he started out. Little soft clouds played happily in a blue sky, skipping from time to time in front of the sun as if they had come to put it out, and then sliding away suddenly so that the next might have his turn. Through them and between them the sun shone bravely ; and a copse which had worn its firs all the year round seemed old and dowdy now beside the new green lace which the beeches had put on so prettily.

Through copse and spinney marched Bear; down open slopes of gorse and heather, over rocky beds of streams, up steep banks of sandstone into the heather again; and so at last, tired and hungry, to the Hundred Acre Wood. For it was in the Hundred Acre Wood that Owl lived.

'And if anyone knows anything about anything,' said Bear to himself, 'it's Owl who knows something about something,' he said, 'or my name's not Winnie-the-Pooh,' he said. 'Which it is,' he added. 'So there you are.'

Owl lived at The Chestnuts, an old-world residence of great charm, which was grander than anybody else's, or seemed so to Bear, because it had both a knocker *and* a bell-pull. Underneath the knocker there was a notice which said:

PLES RING IF AN RNSER IS REQIRD.

Underneath the bell-pull there was a notice which said:

PLEZ CNOKE IF AN RNSR IS NOT REQID.

These notices had been written by Christopher Robin, who was the only one in the forest who could spell; for Owl, wise though he was in

many ways, able to read and write and spell his own name WOL, yet somehow went all to pieces over delicate words like MEASLES and BUTTEREDTOAST.

Winnie-the-Pooh read the two notices very carefully, first from left to right, and afterwards, in case he had missed some of it, from right to left. Then, to make quite sure, he knocked and pulled the knocker, and he pulled and knocked the bell-rope, and he called out in a very loud voice, ' Owl ! I require an answer ! It's Bear speaking.' And the door opened, and Owl looked out.

' Hallo, Pooh,' he said. ' How's things ? '

' Terrible and Sad,' said Pooh, ' because Eeyore, who is a friend of mine, has lost his tail. And he's Moping about it. So could you very kindly tell me how to find it for him ? '

' Well,' said Owl, ' the customary procedure in such cases is as follows.'

' What does Crustimoney Proseedcake mean ?' said Pooh. ' For I am a Bear of Very Little Brain, and long words Bother me.'

' It means the Thing to Do.'

' As long as it means that, I don't mind,' said Pooh humbly.

' The thing to do is as follows. First, Issue a Reward. Then——'

' Just a moment,' said Pooh, holding up his paw. '*What* do we do to this—what you were saying ? You sneezed just as you were going to tell me.'

' I *didn't* sneeze.'

' Yes, you did, Owl.'

' Excuse me, Pooh, I didn't. You can't sneeze without knowing it.'

' Well, you can't know it without something having been sneezed.'

' What I *said* was, " First *Issue* a Reward ".'

' You're doing it again,' said Pooh sadly.

' A Reward ! ' said Owl very loudly. ' We write a notice to say that we will give a large something to anybody who finds Eeyore's tail.'

' I see, I see,' said Pooh, nodding his head. ' Talking about large somethings,' he went on dreamily, ' I generally have a small something about now—about this time in the morning,' and he looked wistfully at the cupboard in the corner of Owl's parlour ; ' just a mouthful of con-densed milk or whatnot, with perhaps a lick of honey——'

' Well, then,' said Owl, ' we write out this notice, and we put it up all over the forest.'

' A lick of honey,' murmured Bear to himself, ' or—or not, as the case may be.' And he gave a deep sigh, and tried very hard to listen to what Owl was saying.

But Owl went on and on, using longer and longer words, until at last he came back to where he started, and he explained that the person to write out this notice was Christopher Robin.

' It was he who wrote the ones on my front door for me. Did you see them, Pooh ? '

For some time now Pooh had been saying

' Yes ' and ' No ' in turn, with his eyes shut, to all that Owl was saying, and having said, ' Yes, yes,' last time, he said, ' No, not at all,' now, without really knowing what Owl was talking about.

' Didn't you see them ? ' said Owl, a little surprised. ' Come and look at them now.'

So they went outside. And Pooh looked at the

knocker and the notice below it, and he looked at the bell-rope and the notice below it, and the more he looked at the bell-rope, the more he felt that he had seen something like it, somewhere else, sometime before.

' Handsome bell-rope, isn't it ? ' said Owl.

Pooh nodded.

' It reminds me of something,' he said, ' but I can't think what. Where did you get it ? '

' I just came across it in the Forest. It was hanging over a bush, and I thought at first somebody lived there, so I rang it, and nothing happened, and then I rang it again very loudly, and it came off in my hand, and as nobody seemed to want it, I took it home, and——'

' Owl,' said Pooh solemnly, ' you made a mistake. Somebody did want it.'

' Who ? '

' Eeyore. My dear friend Eeyore. He was— he was fond of it.'

' Fond of it ? '

' Attached to it,' said Winnie-the-Pooh sadly.

.   .   .   .   .

So with these words he unhooked it, and carried it back to Eeyore ; and when Christopher Robin had nailed it on in its right place again, Eeyore frisked about the forest, waving his tail so happily that Winnie-the-Pooh came

all over funny, and had to hurry home for a little snack of something to sustain him. And,

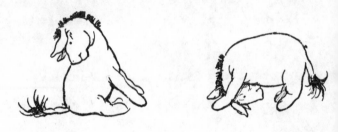

wiping his mouth half an hour afterwards, he sang to himself proudly :

Who found the Tail ?
   ' I,' said Pooh,
' At a quarter to two
   (Only it was quarter to eleven really),
I found the Tail ! '

AT THE ZOO

THERE are lions and roaring tigers, and enormous
    camels and things,
There are biffalo-buffalo-bisons, and a great big
    bear with wings,

There's a sort of a tiny potamus, and a tiny
    nosserus too—
But *I* gave buns to the elephant when *I* went
    down to the Zoo!

There are badgers and bidgers and bodgers, and
    a Superintendent's House,
There are masses of goats, and a Polar, and
    different kinds of mouse,
And I think there's a sort of a something which
    is called a wallaboo—
But *I* gave buns to the elephant when *I* went
    down to the Zoo!

If you try to talk to the bison he never quite
  understands ;
You can't shake hands with a mingo—he doesn't
  like shaking hands.
And lions and roaring tigers *hate* saying, ' How
  do you do ? '—
But *I* give buns to the elephant when *I* go down
  to the Zoo !

THE THREE FOXES

ONCE upon a time there were three little foxes
Who didn't wear stockings, and they didn't wear
  sockses,
But they all had handkerchiefs to blow their
  noses,
And they kept their handkerchiefs in cardboard
  boxes.

They lived in the forest in three little houses,
And they didn't wear coats, and they didn't wear
  trousies.
They ran through the woods on their little bare
  tootsies,
And they played ' Touch last ' with a family of
  mouses.

They didn't go shopping in the High Street
      shopses,
But caught what they wanted in the woods and
      copses.
They all went fishing, and they caught three
      wormses,
They went out hunting, and they caught three
      wopses.

They went to a Fair, and they all won prizes—
Three plum-puddingses and three mince-pieses.
They rode on elephants and swang on swingses,
And hit three coco-nuts at coco-nut shieses.

That's all that I know of the three little foxes
Who kept their handkerchiefs in cardboard boxes.
They lived in the forest in three little houses,
But they didn't wear coats and they didn't wear
      trousies,
And they didn't wear stockings and they didn't
      wear sockses.

THE LITTLE BLACK HEN

BERRYMAN and Baxter,
    Prettiboy and Penn
And old Farmer Middleton
    Are five big men . . .
And all of them were after
    The Little Black Hen.

She ran quickly,
    They ran fast ;
Baxter was first, and
    Berryman was last.
I sat and watched
    By the old plum-tree . . .
She squawked through the hedge
    And she came to me.

The Little Black Hen
    Said ' Oh, it's you ! '
I said, ' Thank you,
    How do you do ?
And please will you tell me,
    Little Black Hen,
What did they want,
    Those five big men ? '

The Little Black Hen
    She said to me :
' They want me to lay them
    An egg for tea.

If they were Emperors,
  If they were Kings,
I'm much too busy
  To lay them things.'

' I'm not a King
  And I haven't a crown ;
I climb up trees,
  And I tumble down.
I can shut one eye,
  I can count to ten,
So lay me an egg, please,
  Little Black Hen.'

The Little Black Hen said,
  ' What will you pay,
If I lay you an egg
  For Easter Day ? '

' I'll give you a Please
    And a How-do-you-do,
I'll show you the Bear
    Who lives in the Zoo,
I'll show you the nettle-place
    On my leg,
If you'll lay me a great big
    Eastery egg.'

The Little Black Hen
    Said ' I don't care
For a How-do-you-do
    Or a Big-brown-bear,
But I'll lay you a beautiful
    Eastery egg,
If you'll show me the nettle-place
    On your leg.'

I showed her the place
    Where I had my sting.
She touched it gently
    With one black wing.
' Nettles don't hurt
    If you count to ten.
And now for the egg,'
    Said the Little Black Hen.

When I wake up
    On Easter Day,
I shall see my egg
    She's promised to lay.
If I were Emperors,
    If I were Kings,
It couldn't be fuller
    Of wonderful things.

Berryman and Baxter,
    Prettiboy and Penn,
And old Farmer Middleton
    Are five big men.
All of them are wanting
    An egg for their tea,

But the Little Black Hen is much too busy,
The Little Black Hen is *much* too busy,
The Little Black Hen is MUCH too busy . . ,
   She's laying my egg for me!

IN WHICH KANGA AND BABY ROO COME TO THE FOREST, AND PIGLET HAS A BATH

NOBODY seemed to know where they came from, but there they were in the Forest: Kanga and Baby Roo. When Pooh asked Christopher Robin, ' How did they come here ? ' Christopher Robin said, ' In the Usual Way, if you know what I mean, Pooh,' and Pooh, who didn't, said ' Oh ! ' Then he nodded his head twice and said, ' In the Usual Way. Ah ! ' Then he went to call upon his friend Piglet to see what *he* thought about it. And at Piglet's house he found Rabbit. So they all talked about it together.

' What I don't like about it is this,' said Rabbit. ' Here are we—you, Pooh, and you, Piglet, and Me—and suddenly——'

' And Eeyore,' said Pooh.

' And Eeyore—and then suddenly——'

' And Owl,' said Pooh.

' And Owl—and then all of a sudden——'

' Oh, and Eeyore,' said Pooh. ' I was forgetting *him*.'

' Here—we—are,' said Rabbit very slowly and carefully, ' all—of—us, and then, suddenly, we wake up one morning, and what do we find ? We find a Strange Animal among us.   An animal of whom we have never even heard before !   An animal who carries her family about with her in her pocket !   Suppose *I* carried *my* family about with me in *my* pocket, how many pockets should I want ? '

' Sixteen,' said Piglet.

' Seventeen, isn't it ? ' said Rabbit.   'And one more for a handkerchief—that's eighteen. Eighteen pockets in one suit !   I haven't time.'

There was a long and thoughtful silence . . . and then Pooh, who had been frowning very hard for some minutes, said : '*I* make it fifteen.'

' What ? ' said Rabbit.

' Fifteen.'

' Fifteen what ? '

' Your family.'

' What about them ? '

Pooh rubbed his nose and said that he thought Rabbit had been talking about his family.

' Did I ? ' said Rabbit carelessly.

' Yes, you said——'

' Never mind, Pooh,' said Piglet impatiently.

' The question is, What are we to do about Kanga ? '

' Oh, I see,' said Pooh.

' The best way,' said Rabbit, ' would be this. The best way would be to steal Baby Roo and hide him, and then when Kanga says, " Where's Baby Roo ? " we say, *"Aha !" '*

'Aha !' said Pooh, practising. ' *Aha ! Aha !* . . . Of course,' he went on, ' we could say " Aha ! " even if we hadn't stolen Baby Roo.'

' Pooh,' said Rabbit kindly, ' you haven't any brain.'

' I know,' said Pooh humbly.

' We say " *Aha !* " so that Kanga knows that *we* know where Baby Roo is. " *Aha !* " means " We'll tell you where Baby Roo is, if you promise to go away from the Forest and never come back." Now don't talk while I think.'

Pooh went into a corner and tried saying ' Aha ! ' in that sort of voice. Sometimes it seemed to him that it did mean what Rabbit said, and sometimes it seemed to him that it didn't. ' I suppose it's just practice,' he thought. ' I wonder if Kanga will have to practise too so as to understand it.'

' There's just one thing,' said Piglet, fidgeting a bit. ' I was talking to Christopher Robin, and

he said that a Kanga was Generally Regarded as One of the Fiercer Animals. I am not frightened of Fierce Animals in the ordinary way, but it is well known that, if One of the Fiercer Animals is Deprived of Its Young, it becomes as fierce as Two of the Fiercer Animals. In which case *Aha!* is perhaps a *foolish* thing to say.'

' Piglet,' said Rabbit, taking out a pencil, and licking the end of it, ' you haven't any pluck.'

' It is hard to be brave,' said Piglet, sniffing slightly, ' when you're only a Very Small Animal.'

Rabbit, who had begun to write very busily, looked up and said :

' It is because you are a very small animal that you will be Useful in the adventure before us.'

Piglet was so excited at the idea of being Useful that he forgot to be frightened any more, and when Rabbit went on to say that Kangas were only Fierce during the winter months, being at other times of an Affectionate Disposition, he could hardly sit still, he was so eager to begin being useful at once.

' What about me ? ' said Pooh sadly. ' I suppose *I* shan't be useful ? '

' Never mind, Pooh,' said Piglet comfortingly. ' Another time perhaps.'

' Without Pooh,' said Rabbit solemnly as he sharpened his pencil, ' the adventure would be impossible.'

' Oh ! ' said Piglet, and tried not to look disappointed.   But Pooh went into a corner of the room and said proudly to himself, ' Impossible without Me !   *That* sort of Bear.'

' Now listen all of you,' said Rabbit when he had finished writing, and Pooh and Piglet sat listening very eagerly with their mouths open. This was what Rabbit read out :

PLAN TO CAPTURE BABY ROO

1. *General Remarks.*   Kanga runs faster than any of Us, even Me.
2. *More General Remarks.*   Kanga never takes her eye off Baby Roo, except when he's safely buttoned up in her pocket.

3. *Therefore.* If we are to capture Baby Roo, we must get a Long Start, because Kanga runs faster than any of us, even Me. (*See* 1.)
4. *A Thought.* If Roo had jumped out of Kanga's pocket and Piglet had jumped in, Kanga wouldn't know the difference, because Piglet is a Very Small Animal.
5. Like Roo.
6. But Kanga would have to be looking the other way first, so as not to see Piglet jumping in.
7. See 2.
8. *Another Thought.* But if Pooh was talking to her very excitedly, she *might* look the other way for a moment.
9. And then I could run away with Roo.
10. Quickly.
11. *And Kanga wouldn't discover the difference until Afterwards.*

Well, Rabbit read this out proudly, and for a little while after he had read it nobody said anything. And then Piglet, who had been opening and shutting his mouth without making any noise, managed to say very huskily :

' And—Afterwards ? '

' How do you mean ? '

' When Kanga *does* Discover the Difference ? '

' Then we all say " *Aha !* " '

' All three of us ? '

' Yes.'

' Oh ! '

' Why, what's the trouble, Piglet ? '

' Nothing,' said Piglet, ' as long as *we all three* say it. As long as we all three say it,' said Piglet, ' I don't mind,' he said, ' but I shouldn't care to say " *Aha !* " by myself. It wouldn't sound *nearly* so well. By the way,' he said, ' you *are* quite sure about what you said about the winter months ? '

' The winter months ? '

' Yes, only being Fierce in the Winter Months.'

' Oh, yes, yes, that's all right. Well, Pooh ? You see what you have to do ? '

'No,' said Pooh Bear. 'Not yet,' he said. 'What *do* I do?'

'Well, you just have to talk very hard to Kanga so as she doesn't notice anything.'

'Oh! What about?'

'Anything you like.'

'You mean like telling her a little bit of poetry or something?'

'That's it,' said Rabbit. 'Splendid. Now come along.'

So they all went out to look for Kanga.

Kanga and Roo were spending a quiet afternoon in a sandy part of the Forest. Baby Roo was practising very small jumps in the sand, and falling down mouse-holes and climbing out of them, and Kanga was fidgeting about and saying 'Just one more jump, dear, and then we must go home.' And at that moment who should come stumping up the hill but Pooh.

' Good afternoon, Kanga.'

' Good afternoon, Pooh.'

' Look at me jumping,' squeaked Roo, and fell into another mouse-hole.

' Hallo, Roo, my little fellow ! '

' We were just going home,' said Kanga. ' Good afternoon, Rabbit. Good afternoon, Piglet.'

Rabbit and Piglet, who had now come up from the other side of the hill, said ' Good afternoon,' and ' Hallo, Roo,' and Roo asked them to look at him jumping, so they stayed and looked.

And Kanga looked too. . . .

' Oh, Kanga,' said Pooh, after Rabbit had winked at him twice, ' I don't know if you are interested in Poetry at all ? '

' Hardly at all,' said Kanga.

' Oh ! ' said Pooh.

' Roo, dear, just one more jump and then we must go home.'

There was a short silence while Roo fell down another mouse-hole.

' Go on,' said Rabbit in a loud whisper behind his paw.

' Talking of Poetry,' said Pooh, ' I made up a

little piece as I was coming along.   It went like
this.   Er—now let me see——'

'Fancy!' said Kanga.   'Now Roo, dear——'

'You'll like this piece of poetry,' said Rabbit.

'You'll love it,' said Piglet.

'You must listen very carefully,' said Rabbit.

'So as not to miss any of it,' said Piglet.

'Oh, yes,' said Kanga, but she still looked at
Baby Roo.

'*How* did it go, Pooh?' said Rabbit.

Pooh gave a little cough and began.

LINES WRITTEN BY A BEAR OF VERY LITTLE BRAIN

On Monday, when the sun is hot,
I wonder to myself a lot:
'Now is it true, or is it not,
That what is which and which is what?'

On Tuesday, when it hails and snows,
The feeling on me grows and grows
That hardly anybody knows
If those are these or these are those.

On Wednesday, when the sky is blue,
And I have nothing else to do,
I sometimes wonder if it's true
That who is what and what is who.

On Thursday, when it starts to freeze
And hoar-frost twinkles on the trees,
How very readily one sees
That these are whose—but whose are these ?

On Friday——

' Yes, it is, isn't it ? ' said Kanga, not waiting
to hear what happened on Friday. ' Just one
more jump, Roo, dear, and then we really *must*
be going.'

Rabbit gave Pooh a hurrying-up sort of nudge.
' Talking of Poetry,' said Pooh quickly, ' have
you ever noticed that tree right over there ? '
'Where ? ' said Kanga. ' Now, Roo——'
' Right over there,' said Pooh, pointing behind
Kanga's back.

' No,' said Kanga. ' Now jump in, Roo, dear, and we'll go home.'

' You ought to look at that tree right over there,' said Rabbit. ' Shall I lift you in, Roo ? ' And he picked up Roo in his paws.

' I can see a bird in it from here,' said Pooh. ' Or is it a fish ? '

' You ought to see that bird from here,' said Rabbit. ' Unless it's a fish.'

' It isn't a fish, it's a bird,' said Piglet.

' So it is,' said Rabbit.

' Is it a starling or a blackbird ? ' said Pooh.

' That's the whole question,' said Rabbit. ' Is it a blackbird or a starling ? '

And then at last Kanga did turn her head to look. And the moment that her head was turned, Rabbit said in a loud voice, ' In you go, Roo ! ' and in jumped Piglet into Kanga's pocket, and off scampered Rabbit, with Roo in his paws, as fast as he could.

' Why, where's Rabbit ? ' said Kanga, turning round again. ' Are you all right, Roo, dear ? '

Piglet made a squeaky Roo-noise from the bottom of Kanga's pocket.

' Rabbit had to go away,' said Pooh. ' I think he thought of something he had to go and see about suddenly.'

' And Piglet ? '

' I think Piglet thought of something at the same time. Suddenly.'

' Well, we must be getting home,' said Kanga. ' Good-bye, Pooh.' And in three large jumps she was gone.

Pooh looked after her as she went.

' I wish I could jump like that,' he thought. ' Some can and some can't. That's how it is.'

But there were moments when Piglet wished that Kanga couldn't. Often, when he had had a long walk home through the Forest, he had wished that he were a bird ; but now he thought jerkily to himself at the bottom of Kanga's pocket.

' If this is shall really take to flying I never it.'

And as he went up in the air he said, '*Ooooooo!*'

and as he came down he said, ' *Ow !* ' And he was saying, ' *Ooooooo-ow*, *Ooooooo-ow*, *Ooooooo-ow* ' all the way to Kanga's house.

Of course as soon as Kanga unbuttoned her pocket, she saw what had happened. Just for a moment, she thought she was frightened, and then she knew she wasn't ; for she felt quite sure that Christopher Robin would never let any harm happen to Roo. So she said to herself, ' If they are having a joke with me, I will have a joke with them.'

' Now then, Roo, dear,' she said, as she took Piglet out of her pocket. ' Bed-time.'

' *Aha !* ' said Piglet, as well as he could after his Terrifying Journey. But it wasn't a very good ' *Aha !* ' and Kanga didn't seem to understand what it meant.

' Bath first,' said Kanga in a cheerful voice.

' *Aha !* ' said Piglet again, looking round anxiously for the others. But the others weren't there. Rabbit was playing with Baby Roo in his own house, and feeling more fond of him every minute, and Pooh, who had decided to be

a Kanga, was still at the sandy place on the top of the Forest, practising jumps.

' I am not at all sure,' said Kanga in a thoughtful voice, ' that it wouldn't be a good idea to have a *cold* bath this evening. Would you like that, Roo, dear ? '

Piglet, who had never been really fond of baths, shuddered a long indignant shudder, and said in as brave a voice as he could :

' Kanga, I see that the time has come to speak plainly

' Funny little Roo!' said Kanga, as she got the bath-water ready.

' I am *not* Roo,' said Piglet loudly. ' I am Piglet ! '

'Yes, dear, yes,' said Kanga soothingly. 'And imitating Piglet's voice too! So clever of him,' she went on, as she took a large bar of yellow soap out of the cupboard. 'What *will* he be doing next?'

'Can't you *see*?' shouted Piglet. 'Haven't you got *eyes*? *Look* at me!'

'I *am* looking, Roo, dear,' said Kanga rather severely. 'And you know what I told you yesterday about making faces. If you go on

making faces like Piglet's, you will grow up to *look* like Piglet—and *then* think how sorry you will be. Now then, into the bath, and don't let me have to speak to you about it again.'

Before he knew where he was, Piglet was in the bath, and Kanga was scrubbing him firmly with a large lathery flannel.

'Ow!' cried Piglet. 'Let me out! I'm Piglet!'

' Don't open the mouth, dear, or the soap goes in,' said Kanga. ' There! What did I tell you? '

' You—you—you did it on purpose,' spluttered Piglet, as soon as he could speak again . . . and then accidentally had another mouthful of lathery flannel.

' That's right, dear, don't say anything,' said Kanga, and in another minute Piglet was out of the bath, and being rubbed dry with a towel.

' Now,' said Kanga, ' there's your medicine, and then bed.'

' W-w-what medicine? ' said Piglet.

' To make you grow big and strong, dear. You don't want to grow up small and weak like Piglet, do you? Well, then! '

At that moment there was a knock at the door.

' Come in,' said Kanga, and in came Christopher Robin.

' Christopher Robin, Christopher Robin ! ' cried Piglet. ' Tell Kanga who I am ! She keeps saying I'm Roo. I'm *not* Roo, am I ? '

Christopher Robin looked at him very carefully, and shook his head.

' You can't be Roo,' he said, ' because I've just seen Roo playing in Rabbit's house.'

' Well ! ' said Kanga. ' Fancy that ! Fancy my making a mistake like that.'

' There you are ! ' said Piglet. ' I told you so. I'm Piglet.'

Christopher Robin shook his head again.

' Oh, you're not Piglet,' he said. ' I know Piglet well, and he's *quite* a different colour.'

Piglet began to say that this was because he had just had a bath, and then he thought that perhaps he wouldn't say that, and as he opened his mouth to say something else, Kanga slipped the medicine spoon in, and then patted him on the back and told him that it was really quite a nice taste when you got used to it.

' I knew it wasn't Piglet,' said Kanga. ' I wonder who it can be.'

' Perhaps it's some relation of Pooh's,' said Christopher Robin. ' What about a nephew or an uncle or something ? '

Kanga agreed that this was probably what it

was, and said that they would have to call it by some name.

' I shall call it Pootel,' said Christopher Robin. ' Henry Pootel for short.'

And just when it was decided, Henry Pootel wriggled out of Kanga's arms and jumped to the ground. To his great joy Christopher Robin had left the door open. Never had Henry Pootel Piglet run so fast as he ran then, and he didn't stop running until he had got quite close to his house. But when he was a hundred yards

away he stopped running, and rolled the rest of the way home, so as to get his own nice comfortable colour again. . . .

So Kanga and Roo stayed in the Forest. And every Tuesday Roo spent the day with his great friend Rabbit, and every Tuesday Kanga spent the day with her great friend Pooh, teaching him to jump, and every Tuesday Piglet spent the day with his great friend Christopher Robin. So they were all happy again.

SNEEZLES

CHRISTOPHER ROBIN
Had wheezles
And sneezles,
They bundled him
Into
His bed.
They gave him what goes
With a cold in the nose,
And some more for a cold
In the head.
They wondered
If wheezles
Could turn
Into measles,

If sneezles
Would turn
Into mumps ;
They examined his chest
For a rash,
And the rest
Of his body for swellings and lumps.
They sent for some doctors
In sneezles
And wheezles
To tell them what ought
To be done.

All sorts and conditions
Of famous physicians
Came hurrying round
At a run.

They all made a note
Of the state of his throat,
They asked if he suffered from thirst ;
They asked if the sneezles
Came *after* the wheezles,
Or if the first sneezle
Came first.
They said, ' If you teazle
A sneezle
Or wheezle,
A measle
May easily grow.
But humour or pleazle
The wheezle
Or sneezle,
The measle
Will certainly go.'
They expounded the reazles
For sneezles
And wheezles,
The manner of measles
When new.
They said, ' If he freezles
In draughts and in breezles,
Then PHTHEEZLES
May even ensue.'

.   .   .

Christopher Robin
Got up in the morning,
The sneezles had vanished away.
And the look in his eye
Seemed to say to the sky,
' *Now, how to amuse them to-day ?* '

RICE PUDDING

What is the matter with Mary Jane?
She's crying with all her might and main,
And she won't eat her dinner—rice pudding
    again—
What *is* the matter with Mary Jane?

What is the matter with Mary Jane?
I've promised her dolls and a daisy-chain,
And a book about animals—all in vain—
What *is* the matter with Mary Jane?

What is the matter with Mary Jane?
She's perfectly well, and she hasn't a pain,
But, look at her, now she's beginning again!—
What *is* the matter with Mary Jane?

What is the matter with Mary Jane?
I've promised her sweets and a ride in the train,
And I've begged her to stop for a bit and
    explain—
What *is* the matter with Mary Jane?

What is the matter with Mary Jane?
She's perfectly well and she hasn't a pain,
And it's lovely rice pudding for dinner again!—
What *is* the matter with Mary Jane?

WAITING AT THE WINDOW

THESE are my two drops of rain
Waiting on the window-pane.

I am waiting here to see
Which the winning one will be.

Both of them have different names.
One is John and one is James.

All the best and all the worst
Comes from which of them is first.

James has just begun to ooze.
He's the one I want to lose.

John is waiting to begin.
He's the one I want to win.

James is going slowly on.
Something sort of sticks to John.

John is moving off at last
James is going pretty fast

John is rushing down the pane.
James is going slow again.

James has met a sort of smear.
John is getting very near.

Is he going fast enough ?
(James has found a piece of fluff.)

John has hurried quickly by.
(James was talking to a fly.)

John is there, and John has won !
Look !   I told you !   Here's the sun !

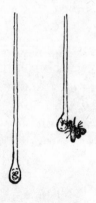

IN WHICH TIGGER COMES TO THE
FOREST AND HAS BREAKFAST

WINNIE-THE-POOH woke up suddenly in the middle of the night and
listened. Then he got out of bed, and
lit his candle, and stumped across the room to see
if anybody was trying to get into his honey-
cupboard, and they weren't, so he stumped back
again, blew out his candle, and got into bed.
Then he heard the noise again.

'Is that you, Piglet?' he said.

But it wasn't.

'Come in, Christopher Robin,' he said.

But Christopher Robin didn't.

'Tell me about it to-morrow, Eeyore,' said
Pooh sleepily.

But the noise went on.

'*Worraworraworraworraworra,*' said Whatever-it-was, and Pooh found that he wasn't
asleep after all.

'What can it be?' he thought. 'There are
lots of noises in the Forest, but this is a different
one. It isn't a growl, and it isn't a purr, and it

isn't a bark, and it isn't the noise-you-make-before-beginning-a-piece-of-poetry, but it's a noise of some kind, made by a strange animal. And he's making it outside my door. So I shall get up and ask him not to do it.'

He got out of bed and opened his front door.
'Hallo!' said Pooh, in case there was any-thing outside.

'Hallo!' said Whatever-it-was.

'Oh!' said Pooh. 'Hallo!'

'Hallo!'

'Oh, *there* you are!' said Pooh. 'Hallo!'

'Hallo!' said the Strange Animal, wondering how long this was going on.

Pooh was just going to say ' Hallo ! ' for the fourth time when he thought that he wouldn't, so he said : ' Who is it ? ' instead.

' Me,' said a voice.

' Oh ! ' said Pooh. ' Well, come here.'

So Whatever-it-was came here, and in the light of the candle he and Pooh looked at each other.

' I'm Pooh,' said Pooh.

' I'm Tigger,' said Tigger.

' Oh ! ' said Pooh, for he had never seen an animal like this before. ' Does Christopher Robin know about you ? '

' Of course he does,' said Tigger.

' Well,' said Pooh, ' it's the middle of the night, which is a good time for going to sleep. And to-morrow morning we'll have some honey for breakfast. Do Tiggers like honey ? '

' They like everything,' said Tigger cheerfully.

' Then if they like going to sleep on the floor, I'll go back to bed,' said Pooh, ' and we'll do things in the morning. Good night.' And he got back into bed and went fast asleep.

When he awoke in the morning, the first thing he saw was Tigger, sitting in front of the glass and looking at himself.

' Hallo ! ' said Pooh.

' Hallo ! ' said Tigger. ' I've found somebody just like me. I thought I was the only one of them.'

Pooh got out of bed, and began to explain what a looking-glass was, but just as he was getting to the interesting part, Tigger said :

' Excuse me a moment, but there's something climbing up your table,' and with one loud

Worraworraworraworraworra he jumped at the end of the tablecloth, pulled it to the ground, wrapped himself up in it three times, rolled to the other end of the room, and, after a terrible struggle, got his head into the daylight again, and said cheerfully : ' Have I won ? '

' That's my tablecloth,' said Pooh, as he began to unwind Tigger.

' I wondered what it was,' said Tigger.

' It goes on the table and you put things on it.'

' Then why did it try to bite me when I wasn't looking ? '

' I don't *think* it did,' said Pooh.

' It tried,' said Tigger, ' but I was too quick for it.'

Pooh put the cloth back on the table, and he put a large honey-pot on the cloth, and they sat down to breakfast. And as soon as they sat down, Tigger took a large mouthful of honey . . . and he looked up at the ceiling with his head on one side, and made exploring noises with his tongue, and considering noises, and what-have-we-got-*here* noises . . . and then he said in a very decided voice :

'Tiggers don't like honey.'

'Oh!' said Pooh, and tried to make it sound Sad and Regretful. 'I thought they liked everything.'

'Everything except honey,' said Tigger.

Pooh felt rather pleased about this, and said that, as soon as he had finished his own breakfast, he would take Tigger round to Piglet's house, and Tigger could try some of Piglet's haycorns.

'Thank you, Pooh,' said Tigger, 'because haycorns is really what Tiggers like best.'

So after breakfast they went round to see Piglet, and Pooh explained as they went that Piglet was a Very Small Animal who didn't like bouncing, and asked Tigger not to be too Bouncy just at first. And Tigger, who had been hiding behind trees and jumping out on Pooh's shadow when it wasn't looking, said that Tiggers were only bouncy before breakfast, and that as soon as they had had a few haycorns they became Quiet and Refined. So by and by they knocked at the door of Piglet's house.

'Hallo, Pooh,' said Piglet.

'Hallo, Piglet. This is Tigger.'

'Oh, is it?' said Piglet, and he edged round to the other side of the table. 'I thought Tiggers were smaller than that.'

' Not the big ones,' said Tigger.

' They like haycorns,' said Pooh, ' so that's what we've come for, because poor Tigger hasn't had any breakfast yet.'

Piglet pushed the bowl of haycorns towards Tigger, and said : ' Help yourself,' and then he got close up to Pooh and felt much braver, and said, ' So you're Tigger ? Well, well ! ' in a careless sort of voice. But Tigger said nothing because his mouth was full of haycorns. . . .

After a long munching noise he said :

' Ee-ers o i a-ors.'

And when Pooh and Piglet said ' What ? ' he said ' Skoos ee,' and went outside for a moment.

When he came back he said firmly :

' Tiggers don't like haycorns.'

' But you said they liked everything except honey,' said Pooh.

' Everything except honey and haycorns,' explained Tigger.

When he heard this, Pooh said, ' Oh, I see ! ' and Piglet, who was rather glad that Tiggers didn't like haycorns, said, ' What about thistles ? '

' Thistles,' said Tigger, ' is what Tiggers like best.'

' Then let's go along and see Eeyore,' said Piglet.

So the three of them went ; and after they had walked and walked and walked, they came to the part of the Forest where Eeyore was.

' Hallo, Eeyore ! ' said Pooh. ' This is Tigger.'

' What is ? ' said Eeyore.

' This,' explained Pooh and Piglet together, and Tigger smiled his happiest smile and said nothing.

Eeyore walked all round Tigger one way, and then turned and walked all round him the other way.

' What did you say it was ? ' he asked.

' Tigger.'

' Ah ! ' said Eeyore.

' He's just come,' explained Piglet.

' Ah ! ' said Eeyore again.

He thought for a long time and then said :

' When is he going ? '

Pooh explained to Eeyore that Tigger was a great friend of Christopher Robin's, who had come to stay in the Forest, and Piglet explained to Tigger that he mustn't mind what Eeyore said because he was *always* gloomy ; and Eeyore explained to Piglet that, on the contrary, he was feeling particularly cheerful this morning ; and Tigger explained to anybody who was listening that he hadn't had any breakfast yet.

' I knew there was something,' said Pooh. ' Tiggers always eat thistles, so that was why we came to see you, Eeyore.'

' Don't mention it, Pooh.'

' Oh, Eeyore, I didn't mean that I didn't *want* to see you——'

' Quite—quite. But your new stripy friend—naturally, he wants his breakfast. What did you say his name was ? '

' Tigger.'

' Then come this way, Tigger.'

Eeyore led the way to the most thistly-looking patch of thistles that ever was, and waved a hoof at it.

' A little patch I was keeping for my birthday,' he said ; ' but, after all, what *are* birthdays ? Here to-day and gone to-morrow. Help yourself, Tigger.'

Tigger thanked him and looked a little anxiously at Pooh.

' Are these really thistles ? ' he whispered.

' Yes,' said Pooh.

' What Tiggers like best ? '

' That's right,' said Pooh.

' I see,' said Tigger.

So he took a large mouthful, and he gave a large crunch.

' *Ow !* ' said Tigger.

He sat down and put his paw in his mouth.

' What's the matter ? ' asked Pooh.

' *Hot !* ' mumbled Tigger.

' Your friend,' said Eeyore, ' appears to have bitten on a bee.'

Pooh's friend stopped shaking his head to get the prickles out, and explained that Tiggers didn't like thistles.

' Then why bend a perfectly good one ? ' asked Eeyore.

' But you said,' began Pooh—' you *said* that Tiggers liked everything except honey and hay-corns.'

'*And* thistles,' said Tigger, who was now running round in circles with his tongue hanging out.

Pooh looked at him sadly.

' What are we going to do ? ' he asked Piglet.

Piglet knew the answer to that, and he said at once that they must go and see Christopher

Robin. 'You'll find him with Kanga,' said Eeyore. He came close to Pooh, and said in a loud whisper :

' *Could* you ask your friend to do his exercises somewhere else ? I shall be having lunch directly, and don't want it bounced on just before I begin. A trifling matter, and fussy of me, but we all have our little ways.'

Pooh nodded solemnly and called to Tigger.

' Come along and we'll go and see Kanga. She's sure to have lots of breakfast for you.'

Tigger finished his last circle and came up to Pooh and Piglet.

' Hot ! ' he explained with a large and friendly smile. ' Come on ! ' and he rushed off.

Pooh and Piglet walked slowly after him. And as they walked Piglet said nothing, because he couldn't think of anything, and Pooh said nothing, because he was thinking of a poem. And when he had thought of it he began :

> What shall we do about poor little Tigger ?
> If he never eats nothing he'll never get bigger.
> He doesn't like honey and haycorns and thistles
> Because of the taste and because of the bristles.
> And all the good things which an animal likes
> Have the wrong sort of swallow or too many spikes.

' He's quite big enough anyhow,' said Piglet. ' He isn't *really* very big.'

'Well, he *seems* so.'

Pooh was thoughtful when he heard this, and then he murmured to himself :

But whatever his weight in pounds, shillings, and ounces,
He always seems bigger because of his bounces.

'And that's the whole poem,' he said. 'Do you like it, Piglet ? '

'All except the shillings,' said Piglet. 'I don't think they ought to be there.'

'They wanted to come in after the pounds,' explained Pooh, ' so I let them. It is the best way to write poetry, letting things come.'

'Oh, I didn't know,' said Piglet.

．　　．　　．　　．　　．

Tigger had been bouncing in front of them all this time, turning round every now and then to ask, ' Is this the way ? '—and now at last they came in sight of Kanga's house, and there was Christopher Robin. Tigger rushed up to him.

'Oh, there you are, Tigger ! ' said Christopher Robin. ' I knew you'd be somewhere.'

'I've been finding things in the Forest,' said Tigger importantly. ' I've found a pooh and a piglet, and an eeyore, but I can't find any break-fast.'

Pooh and Piglet came up and hugged Christopher Robin, and explained what had been happening.

' Don't *you* know what Tiggers like ? ' asked Pooh.

' I expect if I thought very hard I should,' said Christopher Robin, ' but I *thought* Tigger knew.'

' I do,' said Tigger. ' Everything there is in the world except honey and haycorns and—what were those hot things called ? '

' Thistles.'

' Yes and those.'

' Oh, well then, Kanga can give you some breakfast.'

So they went into Kanga's house, and when Roo had said, ' Hallo, Pooh,' and ' Hallo, Piglet ' once, and ' Hallo, Tigger ' twice, because he had never said it before and it sounded funny, they told Kanga what they wanted, and Kanga said very kindly, ' Well, look in my cupboard, Tigger dear, and see what you'd like.' Because she knew at once that, however big Tigger seemed to be, he wanted as much kindness as Roo.

' Shall I look, too ? ' said Pooh, who was beginning to feel a little eleven o'clockish. And he found a small tin of condensed milk, and something seemed to tell him that Tiggers didn't like this, so he took it into a corner by itself, and went with it to see that nobody interrupted it.

But the more Tigger put his nose into this and his paw into that, the more things he found which Tiggers didn't like. And when he had found everything in the cupboard, and couldn't eat any of it, he said to Kanga, ' What happens now ? '

But Kanga and Christopher Robin and **Piglet** were all standing round Roo, watching him have his Extract of Malt. And Roo was **saying,** ' Must I ? ' and Kanga was saying, ' Now, Roo dear, you remember what you promised.'

' What is it ? ' whispered Tigger to Piglet.

' His Strengthening Medicine,' said Piglet. ' He hates it.'

So Tigger came closer, and he leant over the back of Roo's chair, and suddenly he put out his tongue, and took one large golollop, and, with a sudden jump of surprise, Kanga said, ' Oh ! ' and then clutched at the spoon again just as it was disappearing, and pulled it safely back out of Tigger's mouth. But the Extract of Malt had gone.

' Tigger *dear* ! ' said Kanga

' He's taken my medicine, he's taken my medicine, he's taken my medicine ! ' sang Roo happily, thinking it was a tremendous joke.

Then Tigger looked up at the ceiling, and closed his eyes, and his tongue went round and round his chops, in case he had left any outside, and a peaceful smile came over his face as he said, ' So *that's* what Tiggers like ! '

.　.　.　.　.

Which explains why he always lived at

Kanga's house afterwards, and had Extract of Malt for breakfast, dinner, and tea. And sometimes, when Kanga thought he wanted strengthening, he had a spoonful or two of Roo's breakfast after meals as medicine.

' But *I* think,' said Piglet to Pooh, ' that he's been strengthened quite enough.'

US TWO

Wherever I am, there's always Pooh,
There's always Pooh and Me.
Whatever I do, he wants to do,
' Where are you going to-day ? ' says Pooh :
' Well, that's very odd 'cos I was too.
Let's go together,' says Pooh, says he.
' Let's go together,' says Pooh.

' What's twice eleven ? ' I said to Pooh.
(' Twice what ? ' said Pooh to Me.)
' I *think* it ought to be twenty-two.'
' Just what I think myself,' said Pooh.
' It wasn't an easy sum to do,
But that's what it is,' said Pooh, said he.
' That's what it is,' said Pooh.

' Let's look for dragons,' I said to Pooh.
' Yes, let's,' said Pooh to Me.
We crossed the river and found a few—
' Yes, those are dragons all right,' said Pooh.
' As soon as I saw their beaks I knew.
That's what they are,' said Pooh, said he.
' That's what they are,' said Pooh.

' Let's frighten the dragons,' I said to Pooh.
' That's right,' said Pooh to Me.
' *I'm* not afraid,' I said to Pooh.
And I held his paw and I shouted ' Shoo !
Silly old dragons ! '—and off they flew.
' I wasn't afraid,' said Pooh, said he,
' I'm *never* afraid with you.'

So wherever I am, there's always Pooh,
There's always Pooh and Me.
' What would I do ? ' I said to Pooh,
' If it wasn't for you,' and Pooh said : ' True,
It isn't much fun for One, but Two
Can stick together,' says Pooh, says he.
' That's how it is,' says Pooh.

THE OLD SAILOR

THERE was once an old sailor my grandfather
    knew
Who had so many things which he wanted to do
That, whenever he thought it was time to begin,
He couldn't because of the state he was in.

He was shipwrecked, and lived on an island for
    weeks,

And he wanted a hat,

and he wanted
some breeks;

And he wanted some nets, or a line and some
    hooks
For the turtles and things which you read of in
    books.

And, thinking of this, he remembered a thing
Which he wanted (for water) and that was a
    spring ;
And he thought that to talk to he'd look for,
    and keep
(If he found it) a goat or some chickens and sheep.

Then, because of the weather, he wanted a hut
With a door (to come in by) which opened and
    shut

(With a jerk, which was useful if snakes were
   about),
And a very strong lock to keep savages out.

He began on the fish-hooks, and when he'd
   begun
He decided he couldn't because of the sun.

So he knew what he ought to begin with, and
   that
Was to find, or to make, a large sun-stopping
   hat.

He was making the hat with some leaves from a
   tree,
When he thought, ' I'm as hot as a body can be,
And I've nothing to take for my terrible thirst ;
So I'll look for a spring, and I'll look for it *first*.'

Then he thought as he started, ' Oh, dear and
   oh, dear !
I'll be lonely to-morrow with nobody here ! '

So he made in his note-book a couple of notes :
' *I must first find some chickens* '

and ' *No, I mean goats.* '

He had just seen a goat (which he knew by the
    shape)
When he thought, ' But I must have a boat for
    escape.
But a boat means a sail, which means needles
    and thread ;
So I'd better sit down and make needles instead.'

He began on a needle, but thought as he worked,
That, if this was an island where savages lurked,
Sitting safe in his hut he'd have nothing to fear,
Whereas now they might suddenly breathe in
    his ear!

So he thought of his hut . . . and he thought of
    his boat,
And his hat and his breeks, and his chickens and
    goat,

And the hooks (for his food) and the spring (for
his thirst) . . .
But he *never* could think which he ought to do
first.

And so in the end he did nothing at all,
But basked on the shingle wrapped up in a
shawl.
And I think it was dreadful the way he be-
haved—
He did nothing but basking until he was saved !

MARKET SQUARE

I had a penny,
A bright new penny,
I took my penny
    To the market square.
I wanted a rabbit,
A little brown rabbit,
And I looked for a rabbit
    'Most everywhere.

For I went to the stall where they sold sweet
    lavender
(' *Only a penny for a bunch of lavender !* ').
' Have you got a rabbit, 'cos I don't want
    lavender ? '
But they hadn't got a rabbit, not anywhere
    there.

I had a penny,
And I had another penny,
I took my pennies
　　To the market square.
I did want a rabbit,
A little baby rabbit,
And I looked for rabbits
　　'Most everywhere.

And I went to the stall where they sold fresh
　　mackerel
(' *Now then ! Tuppence for a fresh-caught
　　mackerel !* ')
' Have you got a rabbit, 'cos I don't like
　　mackerel ? '
But they hadn't got a rabbit, not anywhere
　　there.

I found a sixpence,
A little white sixpence.
I took it in my hand
  To the market square.
I was buying my rabbit
(I do like rabbits),
And I looked for my rabbit
  'Most everywhere.

So I went to the stall where they sold fine sauce-
    pans
('*Walk up, walk up, sixpence for a saucepan!*').
' Could I have a rabbit, 'cos we've got two sauce-
    pans? '
But they hadn't got a rabbit, not anywhere
    there.

I had nuffin',
No, I hadn't got nuffin',
So I didn't go down
  To the market square ;
But I walked on the common,
The old-gold common . . .
And I saw little rabbits
  'Most everywhere !

So I'm sorry for the people who sell fine sauce-
    pans,
I'm sorry for the people who sell fresh mackerel,
I'm sorry for the people who sell sweet lavender,
  'Cos they haven't got a rabbit, not anywhere
    there !

IN WHICH RABBIT HAS A BUSY DAY, AND WE LEARN WHAT CHRISTOPHER ROBIN DOES IN THE MORNINGS

IT was going to be one of Rabbit's busy days. As soon as he woke up he felt important, as if everything depended upon him. It was just the day for Organizing Something, or for Writing a Notice Signed Rabbit, or for Seeing What Everybody Else Thought About It. It was a perfect morning for hurrying round to Pooh, and saying, ' Very well, then, I'll tell Piglet,' and then going to Piglet, and saying, ' Pooh thinks—but perhaps I'd better see Owl first.' It was a Captainish sort of day, when everybody said, ' Yes, Rabbit ' and ' No, Rabbit,' and waited until he had told them. He came out of his house and sniffed the warm spring morning as he wondered what he would do. Kanga's house was nearest, and at Kanga's house was Roo, who said ' Yes, Rabbit ' and ' No, Rabbit ' almost better than anybody else in the Forest ; but there was another animal there nowadays, the strange and Bouncy

Tigger ; and he was the sort of Tigger who was always in front when you were showing him the way anywhere, and was generally out of sight when at last you came to the place and said proudly ' Here we are ! '

' No, not Kanga's,' said Rabbit thoughtfully

to himself, as he curled his whiskers in the sun ; and, to make quite sure that he wasn't going there, he turned to the left and trotted off in the other direction, which was the way to Christopher Robin's house.

' After all,' said Rabbit to himself, ' Christopher Robin depends on Me.   He's fond of Pooh and Piglet and Eeyore, and so am I, but they haven't any Brain.   Not to notice.   And he respects Owl, because you can't help respecting anybody who can spell TUESDAY, even if he doesn't spell it right ; but spelling isn't everything. There are days when spelling Tuesday simply doesn't count. And Kanga is too busy looking after Roo, and Roo is too young and Tigger is too bouncy to be any help, so there's really nobody but Me, when you come to look at it. I'll go and see if there's anything he wants doing, and then I'll do it for him. It's just the day for doing things.'

He trotted along happily, and by and by he crossed the stream and came to the place where his friends-and-relations lived. There seemed to be even more of them about than usual this morning, and having nodded to a hedgehog or two, with whom he was too busy to shake hands, and having said, ' Good morning, good morning,' importantly to some of the others, and ' Ah, there you are,' kindly, to the smaller ones, he waved a paw at them over his shoulder, and was gone ; leaving such an air of excitement and I-don't-know-what behind him, that several members of the Beetle family, including Henry Rush, made their way at once to the Hundred Acre Wood and began climbing trees, in the hope of getting to the top before it happened, whatever it was, so that they might see it properly.

Rabbit hurried on by the edge of the Hundred
Acre Wood, feeling more important every
minute, and soon he came to the tree where
Christopher Robin lived. He knocked at the
door, and he called out once or twice, and then
he walked back a little way and put his paw up
to keep the sun out, and called to the top of the
tree, and then he turned all round and shouted
'Hallo!' and 'I say! It's Rabbit!'—but
nothing happened. Then he stopped and
listened, and everything stopped and listened
with him, and the Forest was very lone and
still and peaceful in the sunshine, until suddenly
a hundred miles above him a lark began to sing.

' Bother ! ' said Rabbit. ' He's gone out.'

He went back to the green front door, just to make sure, and he was turning away, feeling that his morning had got all spoilt, when he saw a piece of paper on the ground. And there was a pin in it, as if it had fallen off the door.

' Ha ! ' said Rabbit, feeling quite happy again. ' Another notice ! '

This is what it said :

> GON OUT
> BACKSON
> BISY
> BACKSON.
>   C. R.

' Ha ! ' said Rabbit again. ' I must tell the others. And he hurried off importantly.

The nearest house was Owl's, and to Owl's House in the Hundred Acre Wood he made his way. He came to Owl's door, and he knocked and he rang, and he rang and he knocked, and at last Owl's head came out and said, ' Go away, I'm thinking—oh, it's you ? ' which was how he always began.

' Owl,' said Rabbit shortly, ' you and I have brains. The others have fluff. If there is any thinking to be done in this Forest—and when

I say thinking I mean *thinking*—you and I must do it.'

'Yes,' said Owl. 'I was.'

'Read that.'

Owl took Christopher Robin's notice from Rabbit and looked at it nervously. He could spell his own name WOL, and he could spell Tuesday so that you knew it wasn't Wednesday, and he could read quite comfortably when you weren't looking over his shoulder and saying 'Well?' all the time, and he could——

'Well?' said Rabbit.

'Yes,' said Owl, looking Wise and Thoughtful. 'I see what you mean. Undoubtedly.'

'Well?'

'Exactly,' said Owl. 'Precisely.' And he added, after a little thought, 'If you had not come to me, I should have come to you.'

' Why ? ' asked Rabbit.

' For that very reason,' said Owl, hoping that something helpful would happen soon.

' Yesterday morning,' said Rabbit solemnly, ' I went to see Christopher Robin. He was out. Pinned on his door was a notice ? '

' The same notice ? '

' A different one. But the meaning was the same. It's very odd.'

' Amazing,' said Owl, looking at the notice again, and getting, just for a moment, a curious sort of feeling that something had happened to Christopher Robin's back. ' What did you do ? '

' Nothing.'

' The best thing,' said Owl wisely.

' Well ? ' said Rabbit again, as Owl knew he was going to.

' Exactly,' said Owl.

For a little while he couldn't think of anything more ; and then, all of a sudden, he had an idea.

' Tell me, Rabbit,' he said, ' the *exact* words of the first notice. This is very important. Everything depends on this. The *exact* words of the *first* notice.'

' It was just the same as that one really.'

Owl looked at him, and wondered whether to push him off the tree ; but, feeling that he could always do it afterwards, he tried once more to find out what they were talking about.

' The exact words, please,' he said, as if Rabbit hadn't spoken.

' It just said, " Gon out. Backson." Same as this, only this says " Bisy Backson " too.'

Owl gave a great sigh of relief.

' Ah ! ' said Owl. ' *Now* we know where we are.

' Yes, but where's Christopher Robin ? ' said Rabbit. ' That's the point.'

Owl looked at the notice again. To one of his education the reading of it was easy. ' Gone out, Backson. Bisy, Backson '—just the sort of thing you'd expect to see on a notice.

' It is quite clear what has happened, my dear Rabbit,' he said. ' Christopher Robin has gone out somewhere with Backson. He and Backson are busy together. Have you seen a Backson anywhere about in the Forest lately ? '

' I don't know,' said Rabbit. ' That's what I came to ask you. What are they like ? '

' Well,' said Owl, ' the Spotted or Herbaceous Backson is just a——'

' At least,' he said, ' it's really more of a——'

' Of course,' he said, ' it depends on the——'

'Well,' said Owl, 'the fact is,' he said, 'I don't know *what* they're like,' said Owl frankly.

'Thank you,' said Rabbit. And he hurried off to see Pooh.

Before he had gone very far he heard a noise. So he stopped and listened. This was the noise.

NOISE, BY POOH

Oh, the butterflies are flying,
Now the winter days are dying,
And the primroses are trying
        To be seen.
And the turtle-doves are cooing,
And the woods are up and doing,
For the violets are blue-ing
        In the green.

Oh, the honey-bees are gumming
On their little wings, and humming
That the summer, which is coming,
        Will be fun.
And the cows are almost cooing,
And the turtle-doves are mooing,
Which is why a Pooh is poohing
        In the sun.

For the spring is really springing ;
You can see a skylark singing,
And the blue-bells, which are ringing,
        Can be heard.
And the cuckoo isn't cooing,
But he's cucking and he's ooing,
And a Pooh is simply poohing
        Like a bird.

'Hallo, Pooh,' said Rabbit.

'Hallo, Rabbit,' said Pooh dreamily.

'Did you make that song up?'

'Well, I sort of made it up,' said Pooh. 'It isn't Brain,' he went on humbly, 'because You Know Why, Rabbit; but it comes to me sometimes.'

'Ah!' said Rabbit, who never let things come to him, but always went and fetched them. 'Well, the point is, have you seen a Spotted or Herbaceous Backson in the Forest, at all?'

'No,' said Pooh. 'Not a—no,' said Pooh. 'I saw Tigger just now.'

'That's no good.'

'No,' said Pooh. 'I thought it wasn't.'

'Have you seen Piglet?'

'Yes,' said Pooh. 'I suppose *that* isn't any good either ? ' he asked meekly.

'Well, it depends if he saw anything.'

'He saw me,' said Pooh.

Rabbit sat down on the ground next to Pooh and, feeling much less important like that, stood up again.

'What it all comes to is this,' he said. '*What does Christopher Robin do in the morning nowadays ?*'

'What sort of thing ? '

'Well, can you tell me anything you've seen him do in the morning ?   These last few days.'

'Yes,' said Pooh. 'We had breakfast together yesterday. By the Pine Trees. I'd made up a little basket,

just a little, fair-sized basket,

an ordinary biggish sort of
basket, full of——'

'Yes, yes,' said Rabbit, 'but I mean later
than that. Have you seen him between eleven
and twelve ? '

'Well,' said Pooh, 'at eleven o'clock—at
eleven o'clock—well, at eleven o'clock, you see,
I generally get home about then. Because I
have One or Two Things to Do.'

'Quarter past eleven, then ? '

'Well——' said Pooh.

'Half past.'

'Yes,' said Pooh. 'At half past—or perhaps
later—I might see him.'

And now that he did think of it, he began to
remember that he *hadn't* seen Christopher Robin
about so much lately. Not in the mornings.
Afternoons, yes ; evenings, yes ; before breakfast, yes ; just after breakfast, yes. And then,
perhaps, 'See you again, Pooh,' and off he'd go.

'That's just it,' said Rabbit. 'Where ? '

' Perhaps he's looking for something.'

' What ? ' asked Rabbit.

' That's just what I was going to say,' said Pooh. And then he added, ' Perhaps he's looking for a—for a——'

' A Spotted or Herbaceous Backson ? '

' Yes,' said Pooh. ' One of those. In case it isn't.'

Rabbit looked at him severely.

' I don't think you're helping,' he said.

' No,' said Pooh. ' I do try,' he added humbly.

Rabbit thanked him for trying, and said that he would now go and see Eeyore, and Pooh could walk with him if he liked. But Pooh, who felt another verse of his song coming on him, said he would wait for Piglet, good-bye, Rabbit ; so Rabbit went off.

But, as it happened, it was Rabbit who saw Piglet first. Piglet had got up early that morning to pick himself a bunch of violets :

and when he had picked them and put them in a pot in the middle of his house, it suddenly came over him that nobody had ever picked Eeyore a bunch of violets, and the more he thought of this, the more he thought how sad it was to be an Animal who had never had a bunch of violets picked for him. So he hurried out again, saying to himself, ' Eeyore, Violets ' and then ' Violets, Eeyore,' in case he forgot, because it was that sort of day, and he picked a large bunch and trotted along, smelling them, and feeling very happy, until he came to the place where Eeyore was.

' Oh, Eeyore,' began Piglet a little nervously, because Eeyore was busy.

Eeyore put out a paw and waved him away.

' To-morrow,' said Eeyore. ' Or the next day.'

Piglet came a little closer to see what it was. Eeyore had three sticks on the ground, and was looking at them. Two of the sticks were touching at one end, but not at the other, and

the third stick was laid across them. Piglet
thought that perhaps it was a Trap of some
kind.

' Oh, Eeyore,' he began again, ' just——'

' Is that little Piglet ? ' said Eeyore, still
looking hard at his sticks.

' Yes, Eeyore, and I——'

' Do you know what this is ? '

' No,' said Piglet.

' It's an A.'

' Oh,' said Piglet.

' Not O, A,' said Eeyore severely. ' Can't
you *hear*, or do you think you have more education than Christopher Robin ? '

' Yes,' said Piglet. ' No,' said Piglet very
quickly. And he came closer still.

' Christopher Robin said it was an A, and an
A it is—until somebody treads on it,' Eeyore
added sternly.

Piglet jumped backwards hurriedly, and smelt
at his violets.

' Do you know what A means, little Piglet ? '

' No, Eeyore, I don't.'

' It means Learning, it means Education, it
means all the things that you and Pooh haven't
got. That's what A means.'

' Oh,' said Piglet again. ' I mean, does it ? '
he explained quickly.

' I'm telling you. People come and go in this Forest, and they say, " It's only Eeyore, so it doesn't count." They walk to and fro saying " Ha ha ! " But do they know anything about A ? They don't. It's just three sticks to *them*. But to the Educated—mark this, little Piglet—to the Educated, not meaning Poohs and Piglets, it's a great and glorious A. Not,' he added, ' just something that anybody can come and *breathe* on.'

Piglet stepped back nervously, and looked round for help.

' Here's Rabbit,' he said gladly. ' Hallo, Rabbit.'

Rabbit came up importantly, nodded to Piglet, and said, ' Ah, Eeyore,' in the voice of one who would be saying ' Good-bye ' in about two more minutes.

' There's just one thing I wanted to ask you, Eeyore. What happens to Christopher Robin in the mornings nowadays ? '

' What's this that I'm looking at ? ' said Eeyore, still looking at it.

' Three sticks,' said Rabbit promptly.

' You see ? ' said Eeyore to Piglet. He turned to Rabbit. ' I will now answer your question,' he said solemnly.

' Thank you,' said Rabbit.

' What does Christopher Robin do in the mornings ? He learns. He becomes Educated. He instigorates—I *think* that is the word he mentioned, but I may be referring to something else—he instigorates Knowledge. In my small way I also, if I have the word right, am—am doing what he does. That, for instance, is——'

' An A,' said Rabbit, ' but not a very good one. Well, I must get back and tell the others.'

Eeyore looked at his sticks and then he looked at Piglet.

' What did Rabbit say it was ? ' he asked.

' An A,' said Piglet.

' Did you tell him ? '

' No, Eeyore, I didn't. I expect he just knew.'

' He *knew* ? You mean this A thing is a thing *Rabbit* knew ? '

'Yes, Eeyore. He's clever, Rabbit is.'

'Clever!' said Eeyore scornfully, putting a foot heavily on his three sticks. 'Education!' said Eeyore bitterly, jumping on his six sticks. 'What *is* learning?' asked Eeyore as he kicked his twelve sticks into the air. 'A thing *Rabbit* knows! Ha!'

'I think——' began Piglet nervously.

'Don't,' said Eeyore.

'I think *Violets* are rather nice,' said Piglet. And he laid his bunch in front of Eeyore and scampered off.

.   .   .   .   o

Next morning the notice on Christopher Robin's door said:

GONE   OUT
BACK SOON
C. R.

Which is why all the animals in the Forest—except, of course, the Spotted and Herbaceous Backson—now know what Christopher Robin does in the mornings.

THE FRIEND

THERE are lots and lots of people who are
always asking things,
Like Dates and Pounds-and-ounces and the
names of funny Kings,
And the answer's either Sixpence or A Hundred
Inches Long,
And I know they'll think me silly if I get the
answer wrong.

So Pooh and I go whispering, and Pooh looks
very bright,
And says, ' Well, *I* say sixpence, but I don't
suppose I'm right,'
And then it doesn't matter what the answer
ought to be,
'Cos if he's right, I'm Right, and if he's wrong,
it isn't Me.

VESPERS

Little Boy kneels at the foot of the bed.
Droops on the little hands little gold head.
Hush ! Hush ! Whisper who dares !
Christopher Robin is saying his prayers.

God bless Mummy. I know that's right.
Wasn't it fun in the bath to-night ?
The cold's so cold, and the hot's so hot.
Oh ! *God bless Daddy*—I quite forgot.

If I open my fingers a little bit more,
I can see Nanny's dressing-gown on the door.
It's a beautiful blue, but it hasn't a hood.
Oh ! *God bless Nanny and make her good.*

Mine has a hood, and I lie in bed,
And pull the hood right over my head,
And I shut my eyes, and I curl up small,
And nobody knows that I'm there at all.

Oh ! *Thank you, God, for a lovely day.*
And what was the other I had to say ?
I said ' Bless Daddy,' so what can it be ?
Oh ! Now I remember it. *God bless Me.*

Little Boy kneels at the foot of the bed,
Droops on the little hands little gold head.
Hush ! Hush ! Whisper who dares !
Christopher Robin is saying his prayers.

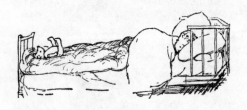